Eugene and His Go-Kart Machine
A tale of a Creative Mouse

By
Lynn C. Skinner

Illustrated by
Polly Rushton

Other books by this author:

Eugene at the Christmas Ball with Christine
The Decisions of a Creative Mouse

Eugene Meets Bojean
The Acceptance of a Creative Mouse

Published by Lynn C. Skinner
PO Box 34 | Alley, Georgia 30410 USA
Cover and Layout Design by Christina Hicks Creative
www.christinahickscreative.com

Published in the United States of America
ISBN: 9780984734405
17.10.31

My husband and I have one grandson, Eric.
We dedicate this book to him.

Acknowledgements

My thanks to all who encouraged me in this endeavor but especially to the Liston females who eagerly waited for the story in print and those who listened and offered suggestions—Alice, Elizabeth, Faye, Katara, Lynne, Truett, and Vedery. Your smiles pushed this offering to completion.

It was spring on the farm. The birds were beginning to sing and the small flowers were peeking through the dirt and showing their first colors.

Eugene, the mouse, awakened from a long nap and lifted his nose in the air. Yes...spring was arriving and he was excited.

All winter he had been dreaming and thinking about the new go-kart in the neighborhood. The boy at the farmhouse down the road had received this wonderful contraption for Christmas. Eugene had watched as the boy whizzed up and down the yard making noise with his toy. Now, Eugene wanted one also.

RainWa

But how could a mouse get a go-kart?

What could he do about this?

He wondered and worried about his problem.
Then he had an idea.

Eugene raced to his pile of treasures. These
were items he found as he scurried looking for
food. There might be pieces that he could
use to build a toy.

cola
cHeese

What do you think he found?

There were several small pieces of wood and bits of wire. Oh yes, he remembered the piece of mirror he found recently. It was shiny and fascinating. He might be able to use it.

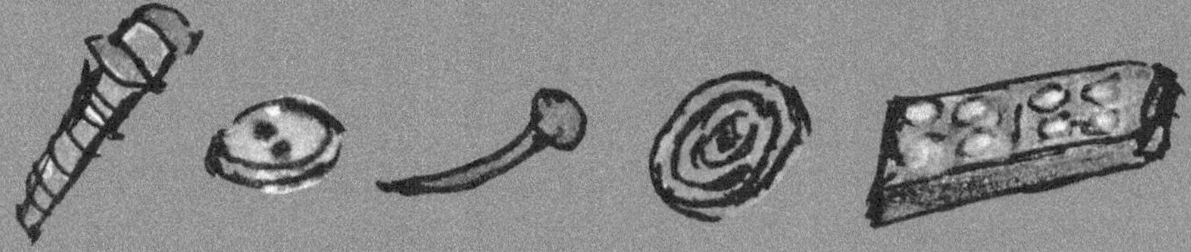

Wheels…yes, he would need wheels. He thought he might have several because toy trucks and cars were constantly losing them. Each time Eugene found one, he carried it to his pile.

Eugene thought a go-kart should have four wheels. Did he have that many? As he looked, he found-not four-but five wheels. They were not the same size, but this was not a problem in the mind of a mouse.

Eugene began to build his toy. He found a piece of cardboard for the base of the go-kart. This would be strong enough to hold a mouse and he attached the wheels.

Next he found a pencil eraser for the seat. Then he added two small blocks of wood for the go-pedal and the stop-pedal. He was pleased with his work.

What did he need now?

He noticed the boy's go-kart had a mirror. He wasn't quite sure why this was needed, but he added his mirror to the back of the frame.

As he tried his go-kart, he realized that he didn't have a way to turn. He searched his pile. Just as he thought this might be a problem too large to solve, he found a small biscuit cutter. He tried it and discovered that it was just what he needed! Next he added his idea of a motor and he was ready for a ride.

Away he went...

around the yard...

behind the barn...

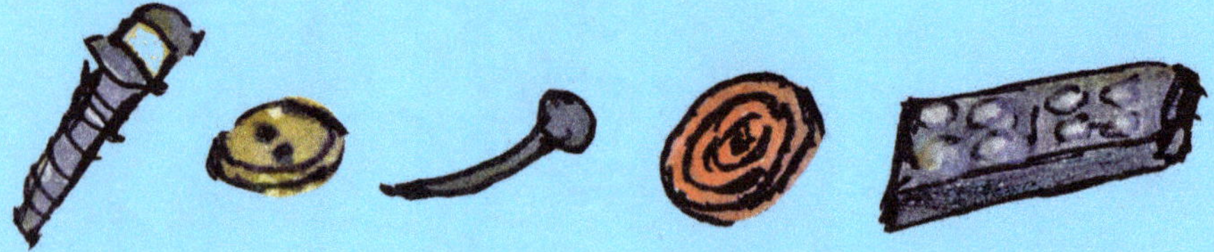

In his excitement, he scared Mrs. Hen and
her chicks.

Then he decided that it would be great to
share his new toy. He hurried to his pile
to find another seat. He drove to the next
farm to invite his friend to ride with him.
They had fun riding and laughing together.

As the sun began to make a beautiful sunset,
Eugene decided that, in his heart, the best part of
the day was sharing with his friend.

Lynn C. Skinner, Author

After completing undergraduate and graduate degrees from Converse College, the author began a typical life of teaching, marriage, children, carpools, lunches and laundry.

It was not until her husband retired that the author began to think in more relaxed ways. Her mind started churning with story lines of character building, creative thinking and problem solving. This story was inspired by her son and memories of his small child play. Enjoy!

Polly Rushton, Illustrator

After moving to Georgia as a war bride, the illustrator began her life as a wife, mother and volunteer. Through her many talents, energy and thoughtfulness, her life has been very busy with projects. She previously illustrated the Uncle Fuddy Duddy series and insists that drawing and painting are just a few of her interests. Her stories and experiences are many.